The Owl Who Asks Why

Michelle Garcia Andersen   illustrated by Ayesha L. Rubio

PAGE
STREET
KIDS

Late at night when all was quiet, Little Owl asked,
"**WHY** don't all animals stay awake at night?"

"Owls don't ask **WHY**," said Mama Owl.
"**WHY?**"

"Owls ask **WHO**," said Mama Owl.
"**WHY?**"

"It's just **WHO** we are," said Mama Owl.
"**WHY?**"

Little Owl continued asking:
"**WHY** is a group of owls
called a parliament?"

"**WHY** can't all birds turn their
heads like this?"

"**WHY** do we regurgitate after eating?"

The other owls laughed when they heard Little Owl.
"**WHOOOOEVER** heard of an owl asking **WHY?**"

Whoo

Whoo

Whoo

Whoo

Whoo

Meanwhile, deep in the woods near the aspen tree grove,
Little Wolf asked, "**WHEN** will I be able to explore on my own?"

"Wolves don't ask **WHEN**," said Papa Wolf.
"Since **WHEN?**"

"Wolves ask **HOW**," said Papa Wolf.
"Not **WHEN?**"

"It's just **HOW** it's done," said Papa Wolf.
"**WHEN** can I ask
WHEN?"

Little Wolf continued asking:
"**WHEN** will I no longer be a pup?"

"**WHEN** is it my turn to be the alpha?"

"**WHEN** do I get to mark my territory?"

The other wolves laughed when they heard Little Wolf.
"**HOOOOW** embarrassing! A wolf asking **WHEN!**"

Hoow
Hoow
Hoow
Hoow
Hoow

Little Owl overheard their taunting.
"**WHY** are you laughing?" she asked the pack.

The wolves howled even harder.

Little Owl and Little Wolf fled
to their favorite tree.

WHYyyy

SQUEAK SQUEAK
SQUEAK

"**WHY** do they always tease us?"
Little Owl asked.

"I don't know. **WHEN** will they understand us?"
Little Wolf muttered.

HOW HOW
HOW HOW

WHEEEEN

With the moon so high in the deep dark sky,
the nighttime melody began.

WHOoo

WHOoo

WHOoo

WHOoo

WHOoo

WHOoo

SCREECH

SCREECH

SCREECH

SCREECH

RIBBIT

RIBBIT

RIBBIT

RIBBIT

TRILL

TRILL

TRILL

TRILL

TRILL

CHIRP

CHIRP

CHIRP

CHIRP

CHIRP

CHIRP

Possum approached Little Owl and said,
"Pardon me, Little Owl, but what's that you say?"

"**WHY.**"

"I just want to know what you said."

"**WHY,**" explained Little Owl.

"Well! I beg your pardon!" replied Possum.

He stomped away, stewing.

Skunk stepped toward Little Wolf and said,

"Little Wolf, what did I hear you say?"

"**WHEN**."

"Just now."

"**WHEN**," explained Little Wolf.

"Oh, forget it!" said Skunk.

He strode away, fuming.

"They'll *never* understand us," said Little Wolf.

"**WHY** do we put up with it?" asked Little Owl.

"I wish we could find a place to ask whatever we want."

"**WHY** didn't I think of that? Let's go!"

"Really?" Little Wolf asked.
"WHEN?"

"Now! Follow me!"

Little Owl flew deep into the forest.

She glided over gullies.

She soared across the sky.

Beneath her, Little Wolf bounded over boulders.

He sprang across the stream.

He climbed the steepest cliff.

Little Owl and Little Wolf traveled all night,
calling out whatever they wanted. But when the sun rose,
they paused. Nothing looked familiar in the daylight.

"I'm tired, and I want to go home," said Little Owl.
"I miss my pack, and I'm a tiny bit scared," admitted Little Wolf.
The two friends were lost.

"None of this would've happened if we asked
the same questions as everyone else," said Little Wolf.

Little Owl sighed, then called, "WHOOOOOO?"
Little Wolf joined in: "HOOOOOOW?"

They hooted and howled as loud as they could,

but they were too far from home to be heard.

"We'll never get home!" cried Little Wolf.

"We can't give up," said Little Owl.
"**WHY** don't we retrace our steps?
WHO got here first?"

"You. It took me forever to climb that . . ."

"CLIFF!" Little Wolf shouted. "I see paw prints!"
"**WHEN** were they made?"
"They're fresh," he said. "They're mine!"
"**WHERE** do they lead?" asked Little Owl.

They followed the tracks to the stream.
"**WHY** do they disappear?" she wondered.
"Because I crossed the water,"
said Little Wolf. "**WHAT** now?"

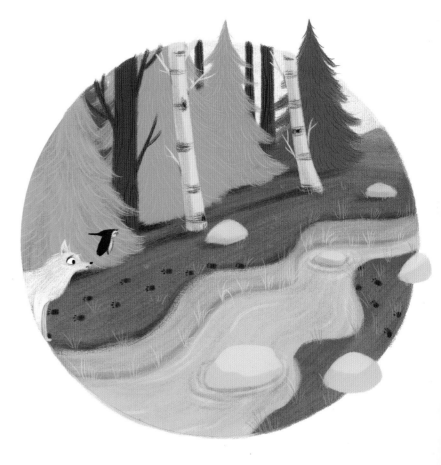

"Look, the boulders!" called Little Owl.

"We're almost home."

"**HOW** can you be sure?"

"Because I see our forest!"

Then Little Owl and Little Wolf heard something familiar.

"**WHO** has seen Little Owl?"
"**WHO** can tell me where she went?"

"**HOW** far did Little Wolf go?"
"**HOW** will we find him?"

"A hoot and a howl!" said Little Owl.
"**WHERE?**" asked Little Wolf.
"Follow me!"

"We were worried about you," said Papa Wolf.
"**HOOOW** come you didn't come home?"

"We were lost!"

"**WHOOO** showed you the way home?"
asked Mama Owl.

"We asked our own questions
and found our way home!"

Mama Owl and Papa Wolf considered this.

Then Papa Wolf asked, "**WHEN** did you become so brave?"
And Mama Owl said, "**WHY** don't you tell us all about your adventure?"

Now when the moon rises high in the deep dark sky,
a new nighttime melody begins. . . .

For Marv, Gabby, Colby, and Rissy. – M. G. A.

To Grace and Robyn with love. – A. L. R.

Text copyright © 2021 Michelle Garcia Andersen
Illustrations copyright © 2021 Ayesha L. Rubio

First published in 2021 by Page Street Kids
an imprint of
Page Street Publishing Co.
27 Congress Street, Suite 105
Salem, MA 01970
www.pagestreetpublishing.com

Distributed by Macmillan, sales in Canada by The Canadian Manda Group

20 21 22 23 24 CCO 5 4 3 2 1

ISBN-13: 978-1-64567-153-4. ISBN-10: 1-64567-153-4

CIP data for this book is available from the Library of Congress.

This book was typeset in Minou. The illustrations were done digitally.
Cover and book design by Melia Parsloe for Page Street Kids.

Printed and bound in Shenzhen, Guangdong, China

Page Street Publishing uses only materials from suppliers who are committed to responsible
and sustainable forest management.

Page Street Publishing protects our planet by donating to nonprofits like The Trustees,
which focuses on local land conservation.

trustees